dick bruna

miffy
at the
gallery

SIMON AND SCHU
London   New Yorl

Mrs Bunny asked the others

– will you come with me?

I'm going to the gallery.

There's lots of art to see.

Mr Bunny said, I'll come

but Miffy's much too small.

Take me too! cried Miffy.

I'm really big and tall.

So off they went together

to view the gallery.

Miffy was excited –

I wonder what we'll see.

First she saw a painting

on the wall above her head.

Said Miffy, it's an apple.

It looks so real and red!

Look Miffy, there's a mobile,

above you in the air.

See how the shapes all balance

as they're hooked together there.

A bear, a real bear, cried Miff.

Oh no, said Mr Bun.

A real bear is nice and soft.

This is a stony one.

That sun is blue, thought Miffy.

I'd paint a yellow one.

And yet a famous painter

painted that blue sun.

I also like these lovely stripes.

To me they seem so good.

But am I looking at it right?

Have I understood?

Look, Miffy, said her father.

That rabbit looks like you.

Don't be silly, Miffy laughed.

I'm real and I'm not blue.

I like that one, cried Miffy.

It's colourful and bright.

Are those shapes cut with scissors?

I think I could be right.

When it was time to go back home,

said Miffy, what a shame.

But never mind. I've seen a lot.

I'm so glad that we came.

And now, when I'm a grown-up,

in just a year or two,

I'll draw and paint and make things.

I'll be an artist too.

Original title: nijntje in het museum
Original text Dick Bruna © copyright Mercis Publishing bv, 1997
Illustrations Dick Bruna © copyright Mercis bv, 1997
This edition published in Great Britain in 2014 by Simon and Schuster UK Limited
1st Floor, 222 Gray's Inn Road, London WC1X 8HB, A CBS Company
Publication licensed by Mercis Publishing bv, Amsterdam
English re-translation by Tony Mitton © copyright 2014, based on the
original English translation of Patricia Crampton © copyright 1997
ISBN 978 1 4711 2077 0
Printed and bound by Sachsendruck Plauen GmbH, Germany
A CIP catalogue record for this book is available from the British Library upon request
10 9 8 7 6 5 4 3 2 1

www.simonandschuster.co.uk